Josie Smith

at the market

Collins

Also by Magdalen Nabb

Josie Smith
Josie Smith at the Seaside
Josie Smith at School
Josie Smith and Eileen
Josie Smith at Christmas
Josie Smith in Hospital

The Enchanted Horse

MAGDALEN NABB

Josie Smith

at the market

Illustrations by Pirkko Vainio

Collins

An Imprint of HarperCollins*Publishers*

First published in Great Britain by
Collins 1995

3 5 7 9 10 8 6 4 2

Collins is an imprint of
HarperCollins*Publishers* Ltd,
77-85 Fulham Palace Road,
Hammersmith, London W6 8JB.

HB ISBN 0 00 185605-7
PB ISBN 0 00 675064-8

Printed and bound by Caledonian International
Book Manufacturing, Scotland

Contents

Josie Smith and Eileen's Baby

Josie Smith in her stockinged feet was watching her mum get ready.

"Can I come to the market as well?" she said.

"No," said Josie's mum, and she looked at her hair in the mirror.

"Why can't I come?" said Josie Smith.

"You always feel sick on the bus."

"I won't feel sick," said Josie Smith, "I promise I won't. Can I come?"

"No," said Josie's mum, and she straightened her eyebrows.

"A-aw!" said Josie Smith. "Go on!"

"No," said Josie's mum. "You feel sick on the bus, you get fed up walking round and as soon as you've been on the roundabout you want to come home." Then she put some lipstick on.

"Can I have some lipstick on then?" asked Josie Smith.

"No," said Josie's mum, and she put the lipstick in her handbag with her purse and the key. Then she put her coat on and said, "Come on."

"I don't want to go to Eileen's," said Josie Smith. "Why can't I go to my gran's?"

"Because there's Eileen as well," said Josie's mum. "Your gran can't be looking after two of you. She gets tired. If you're putting those wellingtons on, take your slippers. And pull those socks up. And button that cardigan up properly. And brush your hair."

Josie Smith brushed her hair. Then she pulled her socks up and put her wellingtons on and forgot to button her cardigan.

She picked up her doll and they went next door to Eileen's.

"I'll not be a minute," said Eileen's mum. "Go in the front room."

In the front room the pretend fire was lit and Eileen's dad had fallen asleep in front of it with the newspaper over his face. Sometimes Eileen's dad worked at night and then he went to bed in the morning and got up for his dinner. After dinner he always went back to sleep with the newspaper over his face.

"Put your slippers on," said Josie's mum. She said it in a whisper so she wouldn't wake Eileen's dad.

But Eileen's dad went, "Wah?" and did a little jump in his chair. Then he went "Hoink—hoink—hoink—sssss," and went back to sleep again.

Josie Smith took her wellingtons off.

"It's wonderful, that fire," said Josie's mum. "The logs and flames are just like real."

"They're not," said Josie Smith, "because you can't throw your toffee papers in it, Eileen's mum said." She went to put her wellingtons on the mat by the back door.

The kitchen smelt of dinner and washing up. Eileen came downstairs. She was carrying her bride doll.

"My mum's bringing me loads of presents," she said. "Some new white socks with a pink stripe round and a bangle and some other things. What's your mum bringing you?"

"I don't know yet," said Josie Smith. "It's a surprise." But she held her doll tight and said it with her eyes shut because she wasn't really having a present. Her mum didn't have as much money for presents as Eileen's mum.

"We've got to play upstairs," Eileen said, "because my dad's on nights and he wants some peace and quiet and the baby's asleep in its pram."

Eileen's baby was fat and white and smelt of cheese and washing powder. Its pram was parked near the kitchen door and Josie Smith looked in it. Eileen's baby was going munch, munch, munch on its dummy but its eyes were shut tight and it was asleep.

"Are you coming?" Eileen said, and they went upstairs with their dolls.

Eileen's bedroom had an itchy pink carpet and a pink frilly cover on the bed.

"Let's play shop," said Josie Smith.

"No, we're not," said Eileen, "because I've tidied my toffee shop set and we're not messing it up."

"Let's play post office then," said Josie Smith.

"No, we're not," said Eileen, "because I've tidied my post office set as well and we're not messing that up either."

Josie Smith was fed up. She liked Eileen's post office set. It had rubber stamps and paper clips and elastic bands and paper and envelopes and a little window to look through and a painting on the lid of a postman smiling and waving. Eileen never played with it properly. She just scribbled on the box and messed everything up and then spent hours tidying it.

Eileen had some toys that she never played with at all. She hadn't even to touch them, her mum said. There was a Spanish doll with a black and red lace frock, and a china puppet with a white satin suit, and a fur dog that nodded its head. They all sat on a shelf in a line and you hadn't to touch.

"Eileen!" shouted Eileen's mum from the bottom of the stairs. "We're off! Now mind you behave yourselves, do you hear?"

"We are behaving ourselves!" shouted Eileen, and she stuck her tongue out.

"Well, see that you do! And don't do anything – *anything* – without asking your dad first! Eileen? Are you listening to me?"

"I can hear you!" shouted Eileen.

"Well, think on!" shouted Eileen's mum. Then the front door went **bang!**

Josie Smith and Eileen waited a minute and then they started giggling.

"We can jump on the bed," said Eileen. "I bet my dad's asleep." She ran to the top of the stairs and said, "Dad? Can we jump on the bed?"

Downstairs, Eileen's dad said, "Wah?" and

did a little jump in his chair. "I'm not asleep," he said. Then he went "Hoink—hoink—hoink—Sssss." And he was.

Josie Smith and Eileen climbed on the bed and jumped and bounced and bounced and jumped and crashed and fell and giggled and screamed until they were hot and red in the face and the bed was all messed up. Then they stopped.

"I know!" Eileen said. "Let's dress up as ladies and put lipstick and powder on."

They ran to the top of the stairs and Eileen shouted, "Dad! Can we dress up as ladies and put lipstick and powder on?"

Downstairs, Eileen's dad said, "Wah?" and did a little jump in his chair. "I'm not asleep," he said. Then he went, "Hoink—hoink—hoink—Sssss." And he was.

Josie Smith and Eileen ran into the front bedroom giggling.

Josie Smith had never been in Eileen's front bedroom before. It had a yellow carpet with straggly bits and a yellow bedspread and yellow lampshades with pleats in them like skirts. The curtains were yellow as well with some more frilly white curtains underneath like fancy underskirts. All the furniture was a pale yellowy colour instead of brown.

Eileen opened the wardrobe.

"A-aw!" whispered Josie Smith. "Those are not dressing up clothes. You'll get shouted at."

"I never get shouted at," Eileen said, "and I can dress up in anything I want."

Josie Smith didn't really believe her, but

Eileen's mum had hundreds of frocks so perhaps it might be true.

"Look at this," said Eileen, and she pulled at the skirt of a long frock. It was deep blue organdie with golden spangles round and a flower made out of cloth at the waist.

"That's a best frock!" Josie Smith said. "You can't!"

"I can if I want," said Eileen. "My mum doesn't care about it anyway because she's only worn it once to the works dance."

"What's the works dance?" asked Josie Smith.

"The works is my dad's factory," Eileen said, "and every year they have a dance."

Josie Smith had seen Eileen's dad's factory once. She tried to imagine all the people dancing in their best frocks round the big frightening machines that roared and smelled of oil, but she couldn't.

Eileen dragged at the frock until it came off its hanger and some other things fell down as well.

"You can put this on," she said, and she gave Josie Smith a long green satin skirt with a lot of sequins round the bottom.

"My mum made this," said Josie Smith. Josie's mum made everybody's best frocks and brides' frocks, too, and Josie Smith hadn't to touch them, not even with one clean finger. Now the green skirt was lying on the floor.

"There's some green satin shoes to go with it," Eileen said and she climbed inside the big wardrobe and started throwing out shoes. She gave the green satin high-heels to Josie Smith and found some golden sandals for herself.

They got dressed up and looked at themselves in the dressing-table mirror. The skirts were too long to walk in so they bunched them up under their arms and Eileen found a gold belt and a silver belt in the dressing-table drawer. Then she said, "Now we'll put lipstick on and perfume."

"And nail varnish!" said Josie Smith. "Let's put nail varnish on as well!" She liked nail varnish best of all and her mum didn't have any. Eileen's mum had heaps, all different colours in tiny bottles with long white glittery handles.

"I'm choosing pink," said Eileen.

"I'm choosing red," said Josie Smith. And they started painting their nails.

It wasn't so easy to do. Eileen bit her nails so

mostly she painted her fingers. Josie Smith painted the nails on her left hand all right but then she got in a mess. The varnish came off while she was doing her other hand so she had to start again and she got a bit sticky. Some of it went on the green skirt but it wasn't so much. Then Eileen nudged her and the red bottle fell over and knocked against the pink bottle and that fell over and a pink and red puddle went on the dressing table.

"We'll clean it up after," Eileen said.

Josie Smith thought it might go hard but Eileen said her mum had a bottle of smelly stuff for taking nail varnish off and they could pour a bit of that on it. So they finished painting their nails and then waved them about to dry. Afterwards, Eileen poured the smelly stuff on the pink and red puddle. The puddle had gone a bit hard but the smelly stuff melted it and they rubbed it hard with some cotton wool and a towel. Most of it came off and the clean patch looked even cleaner than the rest of the dressing table. It came much whiter.

Next they put some lipstick on and some perfume behind their ears and then Eileen opened a drawer with necklaces and rings in it and said, "Let's put jewellery on."

Josie Smith put some big red beads on to match her nail varnish and Eileen put some pearls on and a bracelet.

"Right," she said. "Now we'll go downstairs and have a tea party."

It took them a long time to get downstairs. They had to take their high-heels off and carry them and hold up their long skirts as well. When they got to the bottom they listened at the front room door. Eileen's dad was snoring.

"Dad," whispered Eileen, "can we have a tea party?"

"Wah?" mumbled Eileen's dad and he did a little jump in his chair. Then he went, "Hoink—hoink—hoink—Sssss," and fell asleep again.

Josie Smith and Eileen ran to the kitchen giggling.

"I know!" shouted Josie Smith. "Instead of using your dolls' tea set we can have a real tea party."

"Shush! Don't shout so much," Eileen said, "or

you'll wake the baby up and then we've really had it."

But they did have a real tea party. They couldn't make real tea but they put milk in the teapot and poured it out into real teacups and put sugar in it and drank it. They had sliced bread with red jam on it but no butter. They liked spreading jam more than they liked spreading butter and they could have as much jam as they wanted. They had a lot. They didn't eat their crusts either.

"It's all gone," Eileen said, scraping out the jar with her finger. She had a lot of jam mixed up with her lipstick and a bit down her front and on her pearls. "There is no more red jam, only marmalade."

"I don't like marmalade," said Josie Smith. "I know, let's have a talk like our mums do."

So they sipped at their teacups and Josie Smith said in a grown-up voice, "How are you keeping these days?"

"I'm not too bad," said Eileen, "but I've been on my feet all day and I've got a terrible headache."

"My husband's the same," said Josie Smith. "I've given over bothering. More tea?"

"Just a drop," said Eileen.

"Have you heard about Gary Grimes's Aunty Jane?" said Josie Smith. "They've had to take her away."

"Gary Grimes hasn't got an Aunty Jane," said Eileen.

"It's pretend!" said Josie Smith. Eileen wasn't so good at pretending and you always had to tell her what to say. "You have to say 'Now who's she related to?' And then I tell you."

"Who's she related to?" Eileen said.

"She's related to Gary Grimes's mother," said Josie Smith, "and *she's* related to Gary Grimes on his mother's side. She's been bad a long while."

"My mum's got an ingrowing toenail," Eileen said, "and she might have to go into hospital."

"That's not pretend!" said Josie Smith. Then she got fed up and said, "I know, let's make a cake."

"We can't make a cake," said Eileen, "because I haven't to touch the cooker."

"A pretend cake," Josie Smith said, "with everything pretend. Then we won't get shouted at for stealing sugar."

They ran to the door of the front room and Eileen said, "Dad? Can we make a pretend cake?"

"Wah?" said Eileen's dad, and he did a little jump in his chair. "I'm not asleep," he said. Then he went, "Hoink—hoink—hoink—Sssss," and he was.

Josie Smith and Eileen ran back to the kitchen, giggling. They got out the big mixing bowl and made a lovely mixture of soap powder for flour and a sprinkle of scouring powder for icing sugar and thick yellow washing-up liquid for eggs. Then Eileen got a whisk. She took her high-heels off and climbed on a chair to reach better. It was a whisk with a handle that turned. Josie's mum didn't have one. She beat eggs up with a fork.

"Can I have a go?" asked Josie Smith.

"After," Eileen said, and she splashed the whisk into the mixture and turned the handle as fast as she could.

Slup-a-dup-a-dup-a-dup-whrrup! went the whisk, and a big dollop of mixture slapped on to Josie Smith. "You've spoiled my frock," said Josie Smith. "It's gone all over me."

"It doesn't matter," Eileen said, "because it's soap. It won't dirty your frock, it'll clean it."

Josie Smith washed the mixture off at the sink but she couldn't tell if the frock was cleaner or not because it was wet.

"We should have put aprons on," she said. So they found some aprons and put them on and then it was Josie Smith's turn to use the whisk.

Slup-a-dup-a-dup-a-dup-whrrrup! went the whisk, and a big dollop of mixture slapped on to Eileen's front. But Eileen had her apron on so it didn't matter. Josie Smith carried on slup-a-dupping for a bit but then the whisk wouldn't go slup-a-dup any more.

"There's no mixture left," said Josie Smith, peering into the bowl.

"Of course there is," said Eileen, "there must be. There was loads."

"Well there isn't now," said Josie Smith. "It's gone."

"It can't have gone," said Eileen. "Things get bigger when you whisk them. My mum said." And she peered into the bowl.

The mixture had gone.

"A lot of it splashed on us," said Josie Smith, "so perhaps a bit splashed somewhere else as well." She climbed off the chair and looked around.

It *had* splashed somewhere else as well. It had splashed across the curtains and the kitchen window and then across the wallpaper. It had splashed across the dark red hood of Eileen's baby's pram and the back door and then across some more wallpaper and the fireplace. Then it went across Eileen's front and then the sink unit and a bit more wallpaper and then the window and all the way round again.

"It's gone round in a big circle," said Josie Smith. "We'll get smacked."

"No we won't," said Eileen. "It's only soap. It's clean. Only we'd better put the big dish away because it's my mum's best one. And we'll have to wash it as well."

They carried the big bowl to the sink and put it in the plastic washing-up dish. It was so big it would hardly fit in.

"There is a bit of soap left in it," Eileen said, "but we'll put some more in, in case it's not enough."

Eileen squirted plenty of yellow washing-up liquid into the big bowl and Josie Smith turned the tap on.

"Look!" shouted Eileen. "Look at all the bubbles!"

A huge mound of bubbles came frothing up out of the big dish and all over the sink and the biggest bubbles popped out and floated away round the kitchen.

"We can play with them!" said Josie Smith. "Let's put it back on the table."

But the big bowl full of water was too heavy for them. They tipped a lot of the water out and carried it back to the table between them. They parked it near the edge so they could reach it without standing on chairs.

"Look at them all," said Eileen. "They're everywhere."

The bubbles floated round the room and right up to the ceiling. Big bubbles bumped into smaller bubbles and swallowed them. Little bubbles bumped into the curtains and stuck to them and popped. A shiny bubble bounced off Josie Smith's nose and she blew at it. They both started to blow into the bowl to make more and more bubbles fly round the kitchen and then they chased them.

"I'm getting a straw!" shouted Eileen, "to blow bubbles like in my milk."

She got a packet of straws from a drawer and they both blew into the bowl as hard as they could until the biggest bubble they had ever seen bounced out and floated away.

"It's mine," said Eileen. "I'm going to pop it."

"It's mine," said Josie Smith. "Don't spoil it."

"The straws are mine," said Eileen, "and the bowl's mine and the soap's mine so the bubble's mine and I'm popping it."

"No, don't!" shouted Josie Smith. "Don't spoil it!"

But Eileen reached up her hand to pop it and she pushed Josie Smith out of the way with her shoulder and nearly knocked her down. Josie Smith grabbed the edge of the bowl, trying not to fall, but Eileen pushed harder and popped the big bubble and Josie Smith fell over and the big bowl went crashing and splashing on to the kitchen floor.

Then the baby woke up.

He didn't start roaring, not at first. He just made a tiny noise in his throat.

"Kik-kik-kik-kik."

Eileen ran to the pram and Josie Smith ran after her. They looked in at the baby. He still had his dummy in but he wasn't sucking it. His face was screwed up and red.

"He's going to start screaming," Eileen said. "We've had it if he does. He'll wake my dad up."

"Kik-kik-kik-kik," went the baby.

"Put his dummy in properly," said Josie Smith. "That might stop him."

They tried to put his dummy in properly but his mouth was all screwed up and hard and the dummy just popped out again.

"Kik-kik-kik-kik."

"He's going to start," said Eileen.

And he did.

"Kik-kik-kik-kik-waaaaaaah!"

"He's roaring!" shouted Eileen.

"Give him some jam," said Josie Smith.

"He doesn't eat jam," said Eileen.

"Well, give him some cake, then," said Josie Smith.

"Babies don't eat cake," Eileen said, "and anyway, we have none."

"Well, what does he eat?" asked Josie Smith.

"He chews crusts," Eileen said.

"Well, give him ours."

They gave the baby all the crusts left over from their tea party. The baby stopped crying and started chewing.

"He likes them," Josie Smith said.

"They're for cutting his teeth," said Eileen, "but when he's finished them all he'll start screaming again."

They gave him all the crusts one by one and when he'd finished he started screaming again.

"Kik-kik-kik-kik-waaaaaaah!"

"What else does he eat?" said Josie Smith.

"Sloppy stuff in jars," said Eileen, "with a spoon."

Eileen fetched the jar and spoon and Josie Smith sat the baby up. He looked pleased and hit her on the nose.

"He's supposed to wear a bib," Eileen said, "so he doesn't dirty his clothes." They put a bib with Mickey Mouse on it round the baby's neck.

"I'm not feeding him," Eileen said. "He spits."

Josie Smith opened the little jar and sniffed. It didn't smell much. She got some of the sloppy stuff on the teaspoon and tasted it.

"Waaaaaaah!" roared the baby.

"It's all right," said Josie Smith, "I won't eat it all. Here."

The baby opened his dribbly mouth as wide as it would go and sucked in the sloppy stuff and opened his mouth wide and sucked in some more and opened his mouth wide again.

Josie Smith scooped the sloppy stuff up as fast as she could but it was hard to keep up with the baby. Then, all of a sudden, he got fed up. Josie Smith spooned the sloppy stuff into his big mouth but this time he didn't suck it in. He left his mouth open and the stuff came dribbling out.

"Shut your mouth," said Josie Smith. "It's rude to eat with your mouth open."

But the baby didn't shut his mouth.

"He's going to spit," said Eileen.

"You shouldn't spit," said Josie Smith. "It's rude to spit as well."

The baby stuck his tongue out and the stuff ran down his chin.

"And you shouldn't stick your tongue out," said Josie Smith.

"He's going to spit," said Eileen.

The baby spat.

The sloppy stuff went all over Josie Smith's face and hair and splashed on the fancy pram quilt. The baby grabbed the spoon and hit Josie Smith in the eye with it.

"Ouch!" yelled Josie Smith.

"He's going to start screaming again," said Eileen.

"Don't scream," said Josie Smith.

"Kik-kik-kik-kik."

"What does your mum do," asked Josie Smith, "to make him go back to sleep?"

"I can't remember," Eileen said, "but sometimes I think she sings."

"What does she sing?" asked Josie Smith.

"I've forgotten now," said Eileen, "but she rocks the pram as well."

So Josie Smith sang *Incey Wincey Spider*

and Eileen rocked the pram. The baby was pleased. He clapped and waved and made singing noises. Then the song finished.

"Kik-kik-kik-kik."

"He's starting again," said Eileen.

Josie Smith sang *Sleep Little Bird in your Nest* and Eileen rocked the pram and the baby was pleased but he didn't go to sleep.

Then Josie Smith sang *Old MacDonald had a Farm* and Eileen rocked the pram but the baby didn't go to sleep.

Then Josie Smith sang *Little Jack Horner* and *Lavender's Blue* and *Jack and Jill* and Eileen rocked the pram but the baby didn't go to sleep.

"Kik-kik-kik-kik."

"I don't know any more songs," said Josie Smith. "What does your mum do next?"

"She wheels him up the street in his pram," said Eileen. "He always goes to sleep if you wheel him in his pram."

"We'll have to take him outside, then," said Josie Smith.

"We can't take him out," said Eileen. "If we go out the front way my dad'll see us and we can't go out the back way because the pram's too wide for the gate in the yard and there's a big step as well."

"Kik-kik-kik-kik-waaaaaaah!"

"Your doll's pram!" shouted Josie Smith. "He'll fit in that and that goes through the gate!"

So Eileen got her big fancy doll's pram and they tucked the baby into it carefully. The baby looked pleased.

"He should put a hat on," said Josie Smith, remembering that her mum always said it, "because there's a bit of a wind."

They put a woolly hat with a pom-pom on him and then they put a string of rattles across the hood of the pram. The baby waved and smiled and dribbled.

"I know," said Josie Smith, "while we're wheeling him out my doll can have a sleep in the real pram."

"What about my doll?" Eileen said.

"It's a bride doll," Josie Smith said. "It's grown up. Only baby dolls sleep in prams." She put her baby doll into the big pram and tucked it in nicely. It looked just like a real baby.

"We'll put our coats on," Josie Smith said, "and take shopping bags like ladies."

They put their coats on over their long frocks and jewels and chose a string bag and a basket. They had to put their own shoes on because they couldn't walk in their high heels and push the pram and carry the shopping bags as well.

When they were ready, Eileen tiptoed to the front room door and whispered, "Dad? Can we take the baby for a walk in my doll's pram?"

Eileen's dad went, "Wah?" and did a little jump in his chair. "I'm not asleep," he said. Then he went, "Hoink—hoink—hoink—Sssss." And he was.

Eileen tiptoed away.

Josie Smith and Eileen set off up the street with the pram. The baby smiled and rattled his rattles and then he fell asleep.

"We'll go as far as Mr Kefford's," said Josie Smith in a grown-up voice, "I haven't a potato in the house."

They went to Mr Kefford's greengrocer's shop at the end of their street and parked the pram outside and put the brake on. The baby was fast asleep.

When they went in the shop Mr Kefford looked at them and laughed.

"We're not Josie and Eileen," Josie Smith explained, "we're our mums."

"I see," Mr Kefford said. "Right then, what can I do for you two ladies today?"

Josie Smith and Eileen giggled.

"I thought I'd make a bit of soup," said Josie Smith in her grown-up voice.

Mr Kefford filled their bags with cabbage leaves and leek tops and some old potatoes. Then he gave them each a plum to eat.

"Bye, Mr Kefford," said Josie Smith.

"Bye, ladies," said Mr Kefford.

They opened the shop door and stood in Mr Kefford's doorway sucking their plums.

All of a sudden, Eileen dropped her plum

and shouted, "My mum!"

And Josie Smith dropped her plum and shouted, "My mum!! It's my mum!"

"Run for it!" shouted Eileen as their mums came up the slope from the main road. "Don't let her see you! That's her best frock you've got on!"

They dashed round the corner of Mr Kefford's shop and hid in a gateway down the back.

"We've had it if my mum sees you," said Eileen.

"You said I could put it on," said Josie Smith, "You said!"

"Well," Eileen said, "I never said cross my heart and hope to die."

Josie Smith looked down at the green satin skirt. There was still quite a bit of soapy cake mixture on it and some bits of red nail varnish, and it had got ripped and dirty from trailing along the pavement.

"You said. You said I could put it on and now I'll get smacked!" Josie Smith's chest was going bam bam bam and she was so frightened she felt sick and she hated Eileen.

"My mum'll smack you," Eileen said, "and my dad'll smack you as well."

"I don't care!" shouted Josie Smith. "My mum'll smack you as well!"

"Well, anyway," Eileen said, "you haven't got a dad!" And she nipped Josie Smith hard on her arm and Josie Smith pushed her down and her blue and gold skirt got ripped.

"I'm telling!" screamed Eileen, starting to cry. "I'm telling over you for ripping this skirt and dirtying that one!" And she started running down the back towards home.

"Wait!" shouted Josie Smith, "Wait! Don't tell over me! Wait!"

She ran after Eileen but her long skirt kept slipping down so she couldn't run fast in case she tripped up. Eileen ran in at her own back gate, crying as loud as she could.

Josie Smith trailed slowly home, wiping her eyes on her coat sleeve. When she went in the back door her mum was in the kitchen unpacking the shopping. She looked at Josie and laughed.

"What are you supposed to be?" she asked.

"We've been dressing up," said Josie Smith in a tiny voice.

"I can see you have," said Josie's mum. "What's all that on your face? Jam?"

"Some of it's jam," said Josie Smith.

"Well, get it washed off and set the table while I put the shopping away. I've brought you a present so I hope you've been good at Eileen's."

Josie Smith at the kitchen sink shut her eyes tight and washed her face. She didn't say anything.

Josie's mum unpacked some soap and a tin of talcum powder.

"Take that long skirt off," she said, "and put these upstairs in the bathroom."

Upstairs on the landing, Josie Smith looked across at her mum's bedroom and remembered about the nail varnish on the dressing table at Eileen's.

When she came down her mum unpacked two cups and saucers with flowers on them.

"They're very old," she said, "and one's a bit cracked, but aren't they nice? Put them away in the cupboard."

Josie Smith opened the cupboard where the pots were. She remembered the broken dish in Eileen's kitchen.

"Now where's your present?" said Josie's mum. "I thought it was here – no, that's the vegetables. I thought I'd make a bit of soup..."

Soup! Josie Smith remembered the cabbage leaves. And Mr Kefford's. And...

The baby! They'd left the baby parked outside Mr Kefford's shop!

"I've got to go out," said Josie Smith.

"Out?" said Josie's mum. "You're not going

anywhere. It's teatime."

"I've got to," said Josie Smith. "I've got to ... I've got to take this skirt and these beads back to Eileen's. I promised!"

"Well, hurry up," said Josie's mum, and she put the kettle on.

Josie Smith dashed out of the house with the beads wrapped in the skirt under her arm. At the corner outside Mr Kefford's shop the baby was still fast asleep. Mr Kefford was sweeping out.

"Left your dolly, did you?" he said. "I thought it must be yours."

"It's Eileen's," Josie Smith said. She put the skirt and beads in the pram and let the brake off. She pushed the pram as fast she could down the back and into Eileen's yard. At the kitchen door she stopped and listened. Eileen's mum was shouting but she wasn't in the kitchen. Josie Smith went in. The mess was all still there. She put the skirt and beads on a chair and then took her doll out of the big pram. Very carefully she put Eileen's baby back.

"I'd better take your hat off," she whispered.

The baby opened his eyes. When he saw Josie Smith he started to clap and wave.

"I can't sing for you now," she whispered. "I'll come and sing for you tomorrow if you don't tell over us for forgetting you."

She was so upset that she forgot Eileen's baby couldn't talk.

In the front room, Eileen's mum was still shouting but she wasn't shouting at Eileen. She was shouting at Eileen's dad.

"All you had to do was keep an eye on them! How could you have slept through all that noise? Our Eileen tried to wake you up half a dozen times but she says you took no notice! It would have served you right if they'd woken the baby up, you'd have got no sleep then! If I'm not sick and tired ..."

Josie Smith took her doll and went home.

After tea, Josie's mum said, "Are you coming to sit on my knee for your present?"

Josie Smith sat on her mum's knee and her mum showed her what she'd bought. It was a pair of brand new pure white socks with a sky-blue stripe round the top. Josie Smith loved white socks but her mum always made her wear fawn ones because socks rolled down inside her wellingtons and got spoilt.

"You only wear these with your best white sandals," said Josie's mum. "Are you pleased?"

But Josie Smith wasn't pleased. The new white socks were beautiful, soft and shiny and white as snow, but Josie Smith didn't touch them. She thought of the nail varnish on the dressing table and Eileen's mum's best frock and the broken bowl and the forgotten baby and she didn't know what to do.

"What's the matter?" asked Josie's mum. "Don't you like them?"

"I do like them," said Josie Smith, "but can I not have them tomorrow?"

"Why tomorrow?" said Josie's mum.

"Because I haven't been good today but I might be good tomorrow."

But Josie's mum only laughed and said, "You didn't wake Eileen's dad up?"

"No," said Josie Smith, "but we had a tea party and pretended to make a cake and then—"

"That's all right, then," said Josie's mum, "as long as you didn't wake Eileen's dad. And you didn't touch the cooker or matches or anything else you know you haven't to touch, did you?"

"No!" said Josie Smith, "but when we were dressing up we put nail varnish on and—"

"That's a good girl, because those things are dangerous, you know that. And you didn't wake the baby?"

"We did," Josie Smith said, "and I sang for him and then—"

"That's nice," said Josie's mum, "and did he go back to sleep before he woke up Eileen's dad?"

"He did go back to sleep," said Josie Smith, "but that was when—"

"And what did you sing to him?" asked Josie's mum.

"*Incey Wincy Spider,*" said Josie Smith, "and *Lavender's Blue* and *Old MacDonald* and some other things. But he only went to sleep when—"

"Did you not sing *Sleep Little Bird?*" asked Josie's mum. "I always sang you to sleep with *Sleep Little Bird*. And when I was your age I sang my little sister to sleep with it. Your Aunty Helen. And do you know what happened one day?"

"No," said Josie Smith.

"Well, she wouldn't go to sleep and my mum sent me out to wheel her in her pram to the corner shop. She always went to sleep when she was wheeled in her pram. You were the same. Anyway, off we went and I was as pleased as punch because it was the first time I'd been allowed to take her out by myself. I had to buy a quarter of tea at the shop so I bought that and then guess what?"

"Did you leave the baby outside the shop?" asked Josie Smith.

"I did! How did you guess? You should have seen me running up that street when I remembered! Now then, put your new socks away and get your pyjamas on. It's bedtime."

"But I want to tell you something," said Josie Smith. "Me and Eileen—"

"Don't say me and Eileen. What should you say?"

"Eileen and me — I mean, Eileen and I — but, Mum!"

"All right, that's enough. You've had a good day and now it's bedtime so don't try any staying-up tricks."

"It's not a staying-up trick, honest it's not. I have to tell you something really important."

"It's always something really important as soon as it gets to bedtime. Now, don't let me have to tell you again. Get to bed. And if you behave this week and do well at school I'll take you with me to the market next Saturday and you can go on the roundabout. Not another word, now. Off you go."

Josie Smith went.

When she was in bed in her striped pyjamas she could hear Eileen's mum still shouting at Eileen's dad next door. She felt for her new white socks under the pillow and pulled Percy Panda's big woolly head closer to hers.

"Grown-ups are funny, Percy," she said. "I'll just have to be good tomorrow."

And she was.

Josie Smith and
the Red-Haired Boy

"I hate Wednesday," said Josie Smith. "It's horrible."

"Finish your breakfast," said Josie's mum. "You're going to be late for school."

"I'm telling you something," said Josie Smith. "Wednesday's horrible and, Mum, do you know why?"

"Come here a minute," said Josie's mum, "while I brush your hair. And where's the ribbon to match your kilt?"

"It came out," said Josie Smith. "Mum? Do you know why Wednesday's horrible? Because it's right in the middle of the week and we always have sums nearly all morning and I can't do them and it's always something horrible for dinner and it's always raining so we can't play out. And anyway, Wednesday's a horrible word with stupid spelling. Ouch!"

"If you'd remember to brush your hair before you went to bed you wouldn't have all these knots."

"I did brush it," said Josie Smith.

"Not properly you didn't," said Josie's mum. "You've still got an elastic band in it. Go and clean your teeth and look for that ribbon."

Josie Smith ran upstairs to clean her teeth. Then she found the tartan ribbon to match her kilt in her bed underneath Percy Panda.

"You're still warm, Percy," she whispered to him. "I wish I could snuggle in with you and not go to school at all."

Percy looked at her with kind brown eyes and she covered him up to be cosy.

When she went downstairs her mum took the ribbon and said, "Now, think on. If you don't brush your hair you'll have to have it short."

"I don't want it short," said Josie Smith. "It makes me look like a boy."

"It looks very nice," said Josie's mum. "Nice and tidy."

"It makes me look like a boy," said Josie Smith. "Everybody said."

"Well, see that you brush it," said Josie's mum, and she tied the ribbon tight.

"Mum," said Josie Smith. "Do you know what my favourite colour of hair is?"

"Blonde like Eileen's," said Josie's mum.

"How did you know?" asked Josie Smith.

"Because everything Eileen's got, you want," said Josie's mum. "Brown hair's just as nice."

"Mum?" said Josie Smith, "can I stay at home?"

"Get your coat on," said Josie's mum. "It's ten-to nine."

"I can't do my sums," said Josie Smith, "and there's a test."

"Try a bit harder," said Josie's mum, "and put your hood up, it's starting to drizzle."

The dirty drizzle made tiny dots on the kitchen window and everything looked dark and miserable because it was Wednesday.

"I don't want to go," said Josie Smith. "I can't do tens and units and you said you'd take me to the market if I did well at school and if I can't do my sums—"

"Get your wellingtons on," said Josie's mum. "And remember to put your pumps on when you get to school. And if you can't do your sums, ask Miss Valentine to help you."

"It's a test!" said Josie Smith. "I can't ask her."

"Well, ask one of your friends."

"I can't!" said Josie Smith. "And anyway, there's nobody at my table who can do sums."

"Just do what you can manage and leave the rest like Eileen does," said Josie's mum. "Now, have you got your handkerchief? And don't lose those gloves because you'll get no more."

"But Eileen can't do any of them," said Josie Smith.

"What's that on your face?" said Josie's mum. "Is it sugar? Come here."

"And Gary Grimes can't do them and he spits and rubs out with his finger and makes a hole in his sum book, and Rawley Baxter just plays with the blocks and flies his Batman over them, and Tahara's not at my table any more because she sits next to Ann Lomax, and anyway, she can't do them either, and, Mum?"

"That's Eileen knocking," said Josie's mum.

Eileen was rattling the letter box and shouting, "Is she ready?"

"Go on," said Josie's mum. And Josie Smith had to go.

Josie Smith and Eileen walked up the street to school. They had their hoods up and their hands in their pockets because it was drizzly and cold.

"I'm scared of the sum test," said Josie Smith.

"I'm having a new coat," said Eileen, "on Saturday, from the market."

When they passed Mr Scowcroft's allotment Mr Scowcroft was letting the hens out of their shed. They walked about with stiff little steps, clucking and scratching for worms on the wet ground. Josie Smith stopped to look at them. She liked Mr Scowcroft's hens. They were fat and shiny and orangey-brown. She wished she could give them their breakfast out of the big bin and then stay and play with them. She liked squelching in the mud in her wellingtons and poking with a stick to help them find worms.

"Come on," Eileen said, "or we'll be late."

The bell was ringing. They had to run to catch up with their line going in so there wasn't time to notice that there was somebody new in it. When they got into their classroom, Josie Smith still didn't notice there was somebody new because she was busy taking her wet coat and wellingtons off and putting her pumps on. Then they lined up to go in to prayers.

Gary Grimes pushed in between Josie Smith and Eileen and said, "There's a new boy and I know where he lives and he's got red hair and a two-wheeler."

"Well," Eileen said, "who cares?"

"He can't have a two-wheeler," Josie Smith said, "not if he's in our class. He's not old enough."

"Jimmy Earnshaw's got one," Gary Grimes said.

"What's that got to do with it?" Eileen said.

"He's in Juniors," Josie Smith said, "and he's miles older than us."

"Quiet, all of you," Miss Valentine said.

Mrs Ormerod started playing the piano and they went into the hall. When they were lined up behind the first infants' class, Josie Smith peeped along and saw the red-haired boy. He was tall. He was as tall as Julie Horrocks and she was the tallest in the class. His hair was a dark gingery red and wavy. When everybody was lined up, Miss Potts came marching on to the stage.

They sang a hymn and said their prayers and sang another hymn.

Then Miss Potts said, "Now! Those of you who are having a test today had better make a good job of it. I'm going to check everything myself and if I catch anybody copying I'll have them in my office and their parents will be brought in. Is that understood?"

"Yes, Miss Potts," said everybody.

"Is that understood, Gary Grimes?"

"Yes, Miss Potts," said Gary Grimes.

"What did I just say?" asked Miss Potts.

"You said ... You said ... Is that understood."

"Go to the end of your line!" roared Miss Potts, "and stand next to your teacher where she can keep her eye on you. And I want to see you standing there every morning from now on, do you hear me? And give her whatever it is you're playing with!"

Gary Grimes gave Miss Valentine the rubber band he used for flicking pellets and Mrs Ormerod played the piano and they all went back to their classrooms.

Miss Valentine switched the lights on because it was dark and drizzly.

"Get your reading books," she said, "and read quietly for a minute while I get things ready."

They got their reading books and sat at their tables. Josie Smith read a page and then she had to read it again because she couldn't remember what it said. She was worrying about tens and units. Eileen read her page out loud very slowly, pointing at the words with her finger. Gary Grimes didn't need to point because he only had one word on each page of his book but he pointed anyway and all the words had big black smudges under them. He didn't remember what the words said so Josie Smith always had to help him, but she didn't help him today because she felt frightened. She wished she could only do the story test and spelling and not the sum test. She was good at stories. Rawley Baxter was flying his Batman over his book. He hadn't opened it. Rawley Baxter never even noticed when it was a test. Josie Smith read her page again but she was thinking about the test and about Saturday. Would her mum still take her to the market and let her go on the roundabout if she said she'd tried her best? And what's the use of trying your best if you still get all your sums wrong? It just comes out the same if you don't try at all like Rawley Baxter. And Eileen never tried and she was going to the market and having a new coat as well.

Josie Smith gave up trying to read and looked around. Ann Lomax was giving out the boxes of coloured blocks they used for their sums. Tahara was giving out paper and pencils. Miss Valentine was at her desk writing in the register and the red-haired boy was standing beside her telling her something. Then Miss Valentine looked up and pointed to Josie Smith's table. The red-haired boy came over and sat down next to Josie Smith.

Miss Valentine came over to them and said, "This is Stephen Taylor. Now, Stephen, we're going to do a little arithmetic test this morning and then spelling, and a composition test this afternoon. If you need anything, come to me or else ask Josie here." She put her hand on Josie Smith's head. "Josie knows where everything is and she's very clever, too."

Josie Smith was pleased. When Miss Valentine had gone she smiled at Stephen Taylor because you're supposed to be kind to new children so that they settle in. But Stephen Taylor didn't even look at her. He looked at Rawley Baxter and he said, "What's that supposed to be?"

Rawley Baxter carried on flying his plastic Batman over the skyscraper buildings he'd made with the coloured blocks.

"Der-der-der-der-der-der-der-der Bat-man!"

"I've got one twice as big as that," said Stephen Taylor.

Then he picked up his pencil and wrote on the paper in front of him "Stephen Taylor". Then he wrote "Wednesday" without looking at the date card on the wall to help him spell it. It was scruffy boy's writing but he didn't make a mistake in Wednesday.

Josie Smith wrote her name in her best writing and then she wrote "Wednesday" without looking, but it was wrong. She nudged Eileen.

"Can I borrow your rubber?"

"You're always borrowing it," Eileen said.

"You can borrow it after. I might want it now."

"Go on," Josie Smith said, "lend it me." And she kept her finger over "Wedensday". But Eileen wouldn't. She was like that sometimes. There was nobody else at Josie Smith's table who had a rubber because Gary Grimes used spit and his finger and Rawley Baxter never wrote anything. Ann Lomax at the next table had a pencil case but there wasn't usually a rubber in it. She kept tiny dolls and hair bobbles and toffees in it.

Gary Grimes was writing his name. He couldn't write all of it. He just wrote "Gary" in big wobbly letters that tipped over sideways. Stephen Taylor pointed and laughed. He had big freckles the same colour as his hair and green eyes.

"Shut up, you," Gary Grimes said.

"You shouldn't laugh at people for not being clever," Josie Smith said.

"I'll try not to laugh at you, then," Stephen Taylor said.

Josie Smith, with her finger over "Wedensday", went red.

"Quiet, now," Miss Valentine said. "You can start doing your sums as soon as you get the paper with them on. And no talking or copying."

She gave out the papers and Josie Smith looked at the sums and her chest starting going bam bam bam and she felt hot and sick because they were all tens and units. Josie Smith copied out the first sum but when she drew the line underneath it didn't go straight, even though the paper had squares on it to help you keep tidy. It was because her hand was wobbly.

The first sum said you had to add up 27 and 43. She reached out her hand to get some long blue 10 blocks out of the box but Stephen Taylor's hand got there first and he grabbed the same ones she was reaching for and scratched her hand. Josie Smith got out some other 10 blocks and then a 7 and a 3. When she put the 7 and the 3 on the 10 block they were exactly the same length so that meant she'd made one 10. Under the 7 and the 3 on the sum she wrote 1. Then she was stuck. When you do tens and units you're supposed to carry the tens. Josie Smith didn't know why but she knew you had to. You put one of your numbers down and carry the other. But Josie Smith only had one number and that was 1 and she'd put it down and had nothing left to carry. She took the 3 block and the 7 block off the long blue 10 block and then put them back on again more carefully. She tried nudging them sideways a bit. But no matter what she did they were just as long as one 10. Josie Smith wanted to cry. Why should people have to do sums? Numbers don't mean anything, they just frighten you and they never do what you want them to do, they just do what they feel like no matter how mad you get at them.

Josie Smith looked at Eileen. Eileen was copying out all the sums carefully without doing them. Gary Grimes had only copied out two and he was drawing an aeroplane on the table. Rawley Baxter had built a coloured wall and his Batman was standing on top of it ready to jump off and fly away. Josie Smith looked out of the window. It was still drizzly and dark and they wouldn't be allowed to go out at playtime.

Her tummy started rumbling. She hadn't finished her breakfast and now she was hungry. She wondered what was for dinner. It was never anything good on Wednesdays. Sometimes on Thursdays they had roast meat and roast potatoes. Josie Smith liked roast potatoes. She liked mashed potatoes as well, like they had with baked beans and spam, but that was always on Mondays. Josie Smith thought about baked beans and mashed potatoes and then she thought about baked beans on toast and then she thought about toast with the butter all melted and a lot of red jam. She got so hungry she had a pain in her tummy and the next sum said 19 and 19.

Josie Smith copied it out, keeping one finger of her left hand over "Wedensday" so that Stephen Taylor couldn't see it. She peeped at him. He was writing fast and he put the blocks together fast, and sometimes he did a sum without using the blocks at all. He didn't care a bit about keeping the numbers inside the squares like Miss Valentine said. His numbers were scruffy like his writing but he'd finished nearly half the sums.

Josie Smith got two 9 blocks to help her add up 19 and 19. They were as long as one 10 block and an 8 block. Josie Smith wrote the 8 down under the units side and carried one 10. When she'd finished the sum it looked all right but you could never be sure with sums. Her answer was 38 but how did you know if it was true? She tried another one and then a few more but then all of a sudden her chest started going bam bam bam! Had she put down the units and carried the tens or had she put down the tens and carried the units? And which had Miss Valentine told her to do, anyway? She got so frightened she couldn't remember. She looked at all the sums she'd done. What if they were all wrong?

Stephen Taylor was turning his paper over and starting a sum on the other side. Josie Smith turned over too. 26 + 15 wrote Stephen Taylor in his horrible scruffy writing.

26 + 15 wrote Josie Smith nicely. Then she stopped. You shouldn't copy. Josie Smith stared at the sum and she hated it. She hated all numbers. She tried to make them do what they were told but they wouldn't. They were worse than Rawley Baxter. He always did what he felt like as well, but you didn't have to bother with him. Rawley Baxter had his head down on the table and he was looking sideways at his Batman flying low over the paper with sums on it.

Stephen Taylor was getting blocks out.

Josie Smith got blocks out.

Stephen Taylor wrote a 3 under the units and another 3 under the tens.

Josie Smith wrote the same.

"I'm copying," she thought. But even though she thought she shouldn't she still did. She was so hungry and tired and fed up that she didn't care.

Stephen Taylor got a 10 block and a 7 and another 10 and a 6.

Josie Smith got the same.

"Miss Potts will make me go to her office and she'll tell my mum," thought Josie Smith. But she was so hungry and tired and fed up that she didn't care.

Then the bell went and Miss Valentine collected the papers.

It was hardly raining at all so they put their coats on and went out in the yard. Josie Smith and Eileen walked round and round in the wet eating jelly babies. Eileen ate the black one because they were her jelly babies. Josie Smith didn't care so much because she had tummy ache. The boys were playing football and Gary Grimes ran up to Josie Smith and Eileen with his face all red and his nose running.

"I'm playing with Stephen Taylor," he said, "and he says you must be stupid if you think you're clever because you can't even spell!"

"Oh yes I can spell!" shouted Josie Smith. Then she remembered that she'd written "Wedensday" and she went red.

"Anyway, *you* can't even write your name!" Eileen said, "and anyway, we don't care who you're playing with because we don't want you to play with us."

Gary Grimes wiped his nose on his sleeve and ran off. Then it started raining again and the whistle blew.

After play, Miss Valentine collected all their reading books ready for the spelling test. Everybody had to come out and write one of the words from their reading book on the little blackboard and easel next to Miss Valentine's desk.

When it was Gary Grimes's turn he had to write "House". He dashed up to the little blackboard and wrote HOUS, making the chalk squeak. Miss Valentine waited a bit to see if he would write anything else. Then she gave him his reading book back and he ran back to his chair.

"That's not right," whispered Josie Smith.

"I don't care," Gary Grimes said.

Stephen Taylor laughed.

"Quiet, now," Miss Valentine said, and then Eileen went out to the blackboard.

"Spell 'laugh', Eileen," Miss Valentine said.

Eileen chalked in big letters LAUGH and then she stopped. Then she chalked F. Miss Valentine always told her that GH could say F just as well as a real F but Eileen thought she should put a real F as well, just in case, because it was a test.

"Rawley Baxter," Miss Valentine said next, and Rawley Baxter went out.

"Can you write 'ball' for me?" Miss Valentine said.

"No," said Rawley Baxter. Everybody watched him to see what he would do. Once, when Miss Potts tried to make him write something he kicked her.

"Just try," Miss Valentine said.

Rawley Baxter didn't kick. He chalked some squiggles on the board, pretending to write.

"Thank you, Rawley," Miss Valentine said, and Rawley Baxter sat down.

"That's not proper writing," Eileen said.

"I don't care," Rawley Baxter said.

Stephen Taylor laughed and laughed.

"Quiet, now," Miss Valentine said, and Josie

Smith went out to the blackboard.

"Spell elephant," Miss Valentine said.

ELE wrote Josie Smith, then PHANT.

"Good girl," Miss Valentine said. "It's a word as long as an elephant's trunk but you got it right."

Josie Smith laughed and went back to her place.

"It's a hard word, elephant," Eileen said.

"No, it's not," Josie Smith said, "it's easy."

"Show-off!" Stephen Taylor said, then he went out to the board.

"Now then, Stephen," Miss Valentine said, "you haven't got a reading book yet so let me see. Gary Grimes told me you'd got a two-wheeler bicycle, is that right?"

"I have got one," Stephen Taylor said, "and it's metallic blue and it's got gears."

"Well," Miss Valentine said, "see if you can spell bicycle, Stephen."

Stephen Taylor said, "That's easy." He wrote BICYCLE. Then he went and sat down.

"Very good, Stephen," Miss Valentine said. "I can see you're going to do very well in the test."

"You haven't got a two-wheeler," Eileen said, "because you're not old enough."

"Mind your own business," Stephen Taylor said, "or I'll bash you up after school."

"A-aw! I'm telling over you!" said Eileen. But she didn't tell because the bell went for dinner time and they had cheese and onion pie that was smelly and cold and rubbery, and potatoes like grey lumps. For pudding they had red jelly and a biscuit and Josie

Smith liked that. She ate Eileen's jelly as well because Eileen hated jelly and would only eat the biscuit. Outside it was raining hard and the big windows in the hall were all steamy. They had to stay in their classroom all dinner time and it was hot and noisy so Josie Smith went and sat on the bit of carpet in the reading corner and shut her eyes and thought of a story to write. When the bell went and Miss Valentine came and gave out sheets of paper she was all ready.

She wrote her name at the top, and the day, and started her story.

"Once upon a time" wrote Josie Smith, "there lived a big brown rabbit ..."

She wrote as hard and as fast as she could because she wanted her story to be the best and longest. When her hand started hurting from writing too hard she stopped for a little rest. Her writing looked a bit crooked. Stephen Taylor was looking at it with a screwed up nasty face. Had she spelled Wednesday wrong again? She put her finger over it just in case and then carried on with her story.

"When the brown rabbit saw the white rabbit in a cage, he said ..."

"That's stupid," Stephen Taylor said, "because rabbits can't talk."

Josie Smith's face felt red and hot and her chest went bam bam bam! But she kept on writing her story. Sometimes she had a quick look at Stephen Taylor's paper and his story looked as long as hers. When she wrote faster he wrote faster too, and when she wrote THE END in big letters, he wrote THE END as well. His writing was scruffy, though.

Miss Valentine collected all the stories except for Rawley Baxter's because he hadn't written one.

"Talking rabbits!" Stephen Taylor said when they were putting their coats on at home time. "That's what you are! A talking rabbit!"

When they were going out the gate he shouted, "Talking rabbit!"

And then Gary Grimes shouted, "Talking rabbit!"

Everybody laughed.

When Josie Smith got home she was nearly crying.

"What's the matter with you?" asked Josie's mum.

"Stephen Taylor's been calling me names."

"Wash your hands," said Josie's mum.

"Everybody laughed at me!" said Josie Smith.

"Set the table," said Josie's mum.

Josie Smith set the table.

At bedtime she hugged Percy Panda tight and said, "I hate Stephen Taylor. I hate him and I hate his horrible red hair and I hate his scruffy stupid writing and his stupid two-wheeler bike."

She hated him so much that it hurt her chest and she couldn't even cry.

The next morning, just as they were going past Mr Scowcroft's allotment in the rain, Josie Smith stopped.

"What's the matter?" Eileen said. "Come on, we'll be late for school."

"I don't want to go," said Josie Smith, and she started crying.

"Come on," Eileen said. "That's the bell."

But Josie Smith got hold of Mr Scowcroft's fence and Eileen couldn't pull her away.

"What's the matter with you?" Eileen said, but Josie Smith wouldn't tell. Josie Smith had just remembered that she'd copied her sums in the test. And today Miss Potts would find out. She pushed Eileen away and started running back home as fast as her wellingtons would go. But at the corner of her house she stopped again. If she went home her mum would shout. If she went to school Miss Potts would shout. If she went to school late Miss Valentine would shout. If she went home and then went to school late everybody would shout.

Josie Smith ran back up to school, crying all the way. She was a bit late but nobody saw, and nobody heard her crying because she didn't make a noise and a lot of people's faces were a bit wet because it was raining.

All through prayers she felt sick and she had to keep putting her head down and drying her eyes on her sleeve.

All of a sudden, Miss Potts looked down from the stage and pointed at Josie Smith's line and shouted, "You! What did I tell you yesterday?"

Josie Smith tried to say "Not to copy" but no sound came out because she was too frightened to speak.

"Well?" roared Miss Potts.

Josie Smith was just going to start crying out loud when, next to her, Gary Grimes said, "You told me to stand at the end of the line, Miss Potts."

"Well, go and do it!"

Gary Grimes went to the end of the line and stood next to Miss Valentine, and they sang *All Things Bright and Beautiful*.

When they got back to their classroom, Miss Valentine said, "Josie, what's the matter with you? Come here."

Josie Smith looked up at Miss Valentine and tried to tell her.

"I cop—" she said. "I cop— I cop— I cop—" But she just couldn't say it for crying.

"Come on to my knee," Miss Valentine said, "and finish your little cry and then you'll be able to tell me.

So Josie Smith finished crying on Miss Valentine's knee with her face against Miss Valentine's soft woolly jumper that smelt of nice talcum powder. Then she told.

"Well, that's funny," Miss Valentine said, "because I didn't notice when I marked your sums. Who did you copy off?"

"Stephen Taylor," said Josie Smith.

Miss Valentine took Josie Smith's sums and Stephen Taylor's sums from the pile of papers on her desk.

"Show me which ones you copied," she said.

Josie Smith pointed. "From here," she said, "right to the end."

"But you got all those wrong," Miss Valentine said, "and Stephen Taylor got them all right." Then she said, "I see what you did. You copied Stephen Taylor's answers but you put them down under the wrong sums. And do you know that, up till then, apart from the first sum, you were getting them all right by yourself? Oh, Josie, what am I going to do with you?"

"I don't know," said Josie Smith.

"If you'd carried on by yourself," Miss Valentine said, "you'd probably have got nine out of ten. Why do you get so frightened, Josie?"

"I don't know," said Josie Smith. "Will Miss Potts shout at me?"

"No, she won't," Miss Valentine said. "She didn't notice like I didn't notice. If you'd got the sums right and done well because of copying I'd have had to tell her. But you've only made things worse for yourself, haven't you?"

"Yes," said Josie Smith.

Miss Valentine took a tissue from the box on her desk. "Another time," she said, "just do your best and try not to get so frightened. Do you promise?"

"Yes," said Josie Smith.

"Blow," Miss Valentine said. And Josie Smith blew.

When she went to sit down, Eileen said to her, "Stephen Taylor says he's going to thump us and I'm telling over him."

Josie Smith didn't say anything. Stephen Taylor was big, and if he found out that Josie Smith had copied off him he might really thump her. She didn't look at him all morning and he didn't look at her. They had chips for dinner and Josie Smith cheered up. After dinner they did drawing and she cheered up even more. She drew a princess for herself and one for Eileen. They were just starting to colour them in when the door opened and Miss Potts marched in with her face all red and shouted, "How dare any of you copy after what I said yesterday!" Then she shouted, "Excuse me, Miss Valentine!" And she waved two pieces of paper. "Where does Stephen Taylor sit?"

Miss Valentine showed her.

"I thought as much," roared Miss Potts, "next to Josie Smith!"

Josie Smith's chest went bam bam bam and she felt sick again.

"Come out here, the pair of you!" roared Miss Potts.

Josie Smith and Stephen Taylor stood up and went out to Miss Potts.

"I'm surprised at you," shouted Miss Potts at Stephen Taylor. "Weren't you the cleverest in the class at your last school? Isn't that what your father told me yesterday morning when he brought you?"

Stephen Taylor didn't answer.

"And you, young lady," shouted Miss Potts at Josie Smith, "did you know about this copying? Well?"

"Yes, Miss Potts," whispered Josie Smith.

"Talking rabbits!" roared Miss Potts. "I'll give you talking rabbits! Your parents are going to hear about this! Thank you, Miss Valentine!" And Miss Potts slammed the papers on Miss Valentine's desk and marched out.

Miss Valentine stared at the papers. Josie Smith stared at the papers. Stephen Taylor stared at the papers. Everybody else waited to see what would happen. Miss Valentine picked one of the papers up. "'Once upon a time there was a rabbit ...'" she read. "It's your story," she said to Josie Smith. And it was. And on the other paper was the same story copied by Stephen Taylor.

"You copied Josie's story," Miss Valentine said.

"I can't make up stories," Stephen Taylor said.

"Did you really know he'd copied it?" Miss Valentine asked.

"No," said Josie Smith.

"But then why did you tell Miss Potts that you knew?"

"I thought she meant my sums," said Josie Smith.

"Oh, for goodness' sake," Miss Valentine said. "Go and sit down and read."

At home time when they were putting their coats on Eileen said to Josie Smith, "I'm not walking home with you because you cheated." Then she went off with Ann Lomax.

Josie Smith set off home by herself feeling a bit frightened. Stephen Taylor was bigger than she was and she couldn't fight him. She started running home and then she stopped. Stephen Taylor was there. He was standing by himself near Mr Scowcroft's allotment and he was kicking at the fence and making the hens run away.

"You stop that!" shouted Josie Smith. She forgot to be frightened of Stephen Taylor because the hens were her friends. "Just you stop it! You're frightening them!"

Stephen Taylor turned round and looked at Josie Smith. His face was nearly as red as his hair, and his nose was running and his cheeks were all dirty and wet.

Josie Smith stopped shouting.

"What are you crying for?" she said.

"I'm not," Stephen Taylor said. But he was.

"Are you frightened of Miss Potts?" said Josie Smith. Everybody was frightened of Miss Potts.

Stephen Taylor shook his head and kicked the fence again. The hens watched him from near their shed. Josie Smith didn't shout.

"What are you frightened of, then?" she said.

"Going home," Stephen Taylor said, "and telling my dad."

"Does he shout?" asked Josie Smith.

Stephen Taylor shook his head

"Does he smack?" asked Josie Smith.

Stephen Taylor shook his head.

"What does he do, then?" asked Josie Smith.

"He gets upset," Stephen Taylor said, "if I'm not the best in the class any more like I used to be. He made me change schools and now I've got no friends."

Josie Smith didn't really know what he was talking about. She hadn't got a dad so she wasn't sure what sort of things they did.

"Why don't you tell your mum?" she said, "and then she'll let you go back to your other school."

"I haven't got a mum any more," Stephen Taylor said.

"But you have to have a mum," said Josie Smith, "or there's nobody to make your dinner and look after you when you go home."

"I can go home by myself," Stephen Taylor said. "I've got my own key and then I wait for my dad to come home from work.

He bought me a video and some new football boots and a bike because my mum's gone away to live somewhere else."

"Is it really a two-wheeler?" asked Josie Smith.

"If I tell you," Stephen Taylor said, "you haven't to tell anybody else."

"I won't tell," said Josie Smith. "Cross my heart and hope to die."

"It is a two-wheeler," Stephen Taylor said, "but it hasn't got gears. It's a mini two-wheeler with stabilizers. If you don't tell my dad I copied off you I'll let you have a ride on it."

"I never tell over people," Josie Smith said, "and anyway, I copied some sums off you. But Miss Potts might tell him. She said she'd tell. And if you want you can come to our house till your dad comes home. I'll ask my mum if you can stay for your tea because you haven't got a mum."

"I can't stay without asking first," Stephen Taylor said, "but I'll see if I can tomorrow." And he stopped crying and they started walking down the road.

"My mum can sew frocks," said Josie Smith. "Even wedding frocks with lace and everything."

"My dad can mend things," Stephen Taylor said, "and he can fish and I can as well. If you want to know how to catch tiddlers I can show you. You have to bring a jam jar."

"My mum's got loads of jam jars," Josie Smith said. "I'll ask her for one when I get in."

"Mum!" she shouted when she ran in at her front door and banged it. "Stephen Taylor's going to come for his tea and he can catch tiddlers and ride a two-wheeler nearly and he can even do sums!"

"Don't bang the door," said Josie's mum, "and I thought Stephen Taylor was the one who called you names."

"I can't remember," said Josie Smith, "and anyway, sticks and stones may break my bones but calling names won't hurt me. And, Mum? Do you know what my favourite colour of hair is?"

"Blonde like Eileen's," said Josie's mum.

"Well, it's not!" said Josie Smith. "It's red! Because a red-haired boy's my friend."

Josie Smith at the Market

Josie Smith and Josie's mum were having their Saturday dinner. All morning it had been raining and the black wall out in the yard was wet and shiny.

"I think it's clearing up," said Josie's mum, looking out.

The wind rattled some more rain against the kitchen window and then the sun came out.

"Can I wear my sandals?" asked Josie Smith.

"No, you can't," said Josie's mum. "You can't wear white summer sandals in this weather. You'll wear your shoes."

Josie Smith hated her shoes. They were hard brown lace-ups and she had to walk carefully in them so she didn't kick the toes in. It was all right walking carefully in white sandals because she liked them. "Can I wear my wellingtons, then?" she said.

"You'll wear your shoes," said Josie's mum, "and if you don't finish that meat you won't go at all. Now get on with your dinner."

Josie Smith got on with her dinner. She didn't feel hungry because she had butterflies in her tummy. She was excited because they were going to the market and there was a roundabout and toy stalls and hot potatoes and hundreds of flowers and new clothes and a man with a suitcase who sold monkeys that ran up and down sticks. If you're thinking about all those things you don't want your dinner but Josie Smith knew a trick to help her.

She watched her mum and ate exactly the same as she ate. If her mum got a bit of potato and carrot on her fork Josie Smith got a bit of potato and carrot on her fork. If her mum cut a bit of meat and looked out of the window while she ate it Josie Smith cut a bit of meat and looked out of the window while she ate it. So she finished her dinner without really noticing, and eating pudding's easy.

"Will we see Christine Penny?" she asked.

"I don't know," said Josie's mum. "We might do. You'll have to wait and see."

Christine Penny didn't go to Josie Smith's school. Her mum sold clothes at the market. If Christine Penny was there Josie Smith could play with her while their mums were talking. They could run in and out between the stalls and hide behind the coats hanging up.

"I like Christine Penny," said Josie Smith.

"You just like her name," said Josie's mum.

"I know," said Josie Smith, "but she's got plaits and a bangle as well. Are we going now?"

"I want a cup of tea," said Josie's mum. "You wash your hands and face and button that cardigan properly."

When they got to the bus stop the wind was blowing and the sun was shining and Eileen was there with her mum.

"I'm having a new coat," Eileen said, "and it's sky blue quilted with a hood."

Josie Smith didn't say anything.

"And do you want to know what?" said Eileen. "There's a stall that sells brooches with your name on them and I'm buying one. Are you as well?"

"I might," said Josie Smith, but she said it with her eyes shut because she only had ten pence and she didn't know how much they cost.

Josie Smith sat with her mum on the bus and Eileen sat with hers. They hated the smell of the bus and its noise and sometimes they felt sick. When Eileen felt sick she cried and when Josie Smith felt sick she went very quiet and pale. Sometimes Josie Smith said it was the grown-ups talking so loud that made her feel sick. They were talking really loudly now and they had big coats and macs and bags and umbrellas and they squashed you in so you couldn't see and sometimes you could hardly breathe.

"Can I sit near the window?" asked Josie Smith.

"You can sit on my knee," said Josie's mum, "and let that lady sit down."

And then she was even more squashed than before but at least she could look out of the window.

When she saw the hospital where she'd had her tonsils out she knew they were nearly there and she wouldn't be sick.

Near the market everybody got off the bus because it didn't go any further. Josie Smith and Eileen had to hold their mums' hands to cross the road. Then they held each other's hands and ran in front. They stamped their feet and jumped and shouted, "We're going on the roundabout! We're going on the roundabout!"

Then Eileen ran back to her mum and said, "Can we go on the roundabout straight away?"

"In a minute," said Eileen's mum.

But they'd only just got past the hot potato man when their mums stopped to talk to a lady with a red headscarf on. They talked and talked and talked. They said, "How are you keeping?" and they said, "Have you heard Betty Scowcroft's in hospital?" and they said, "You remember her, she married that youngest boy of the Kershaw's."

And Josie Smith and Eileen had to wait and wait and wait.

Then they went along by the fruit stalls and bought apples and lettuce and tomatoes. The fruit stalls were right near the roundabout. When a lady with a brown and yellow headscarf came up to their mums and said, "How are you keeping?" Josie Smith and Eileen ran away. They ran to the roundabout and waited there.

"What are you going on?" Eileen said. "I'm going on that white car because it's got a horn."

"I think I'll go on the engine," Josie Smith said, "because there's a bell you can ring. Only, I like the horse as well."

"I'm not going on the horse," Eileen said. "You can fall off it. My mum said."

"Well," Josie Smith said, "who cares if you can?" She had never thought about falling off the horse. There was a boy on it now and he was slipping sideways a bit. He didn't fall off because there was a big pole to hold on to. The horse had a golden mane and a red saddle and his mouth was open a bit so you could see his teeth and he was galloping. But he didn't have a bell. Josie Smith liked the bell. Somebody was ringing it now.

"Look, on the engine," Eileen said. "That's Gary Grimes."

And it was. When the roundabout stopped he jumped off and ran past them crying and shouting, "Mum! Where's my mum? I've lost my mum!"

He hadn't lost his mum. She was on the other side of the roundabout, talking, like Josie's mum and Eileen's mum. She got hold of him and shouted at him for being so soft.

The roundabout man rang his bell.

"Let's get on," said Eileen.

"We can't," Josie Smith said, "without our mums. You have to pay."

"Well," said Eileen, "we can pay with our spending money."

"We can't," Josie Smith said, "because we're buying our brooches with it."

"We can get some more money off our mums," Eileen said, and she climbed on the roundabout and got into the white car.

Josie Smith put her hand in her pocket and felt for the ten pence piece. She didn't know what to do. A little boy got on the horse but when his mum left him he started crying and slipping off it and she had to come back for him. She put him in the space ship and he stopped crying. Then two girls, bigger than Josie Smith, climbed into the engine and started ringing the bell. The roundabout was nearly full.

Josie Smith looked back to see if her mum was coming but they were all still talking near the fruit stall and her mum didn't look at her. Even so, her mum had said she could go on the roundabout. She always let her go on the roundabout. Josie Smith decided to get on. She started to climb up but a big girl pushed her and got on the horse. Now there was only a horrible blue car left round the other side. Josie Smith pushed past the horse and the spaceship to get to it. She didn't want to go on the horrible car but she was on the roundabout now so she didn't know what else she could do.

Then, just when she was nearly there, a boy jumped on from the other side and got in the car. The bell was ringing. What would she do when the roundabout set off and she had nowhere to sit? She'd fall! Josie Smith got hold of one of the twisty coloured poles near the edge of the platform and her chest was going bam bam bam! and the music was starting.

"Oi!" shouted a man's voice. "Oi, you!" It was the roundabout man with his apron full of money. "Get off!" he shouted. "We're full!"

Josie Smith kept hold of the pole because she was too frightened to move.

"Get that kid off!" shouted the man.

Somebody lifted Josie Smith down. It was Gary Grimes's mum.

"What are you doing here by yourself?" she said.

"My mum's over there," said Josie Smith.

Then Gary Grimes's mum went away with Gary Grimes who was still crying, and the roundabout set off.

Eileen honked her horn every time she passed Josie Smith. Then their mums came.

"Where's Eileen gone?" said Eileen's mum.

"She's on the roundabout," said Josie Smith.

"Why didn't you go on with her?" asked Josie's mum. "You said you wanted to."

"I do want to," said Josie Smith.

"All the pestering you do," said Josie's mum, "and then you change your mind."

"I didn't pester," said Josie Smith, "Eileen pestered, and I haven't changed my mind."

But her mum was talking to Eileen's mum and she didn't listen. When the roundabout stopped and Eileen got off, her mum said to her, "Why didn't Josie go on with you?"

"She did get on," Eileen said, "but she was

scared of falling off the horse. I saw her crying and she got off again."

"Come on," said Josie's mum. "I'm surprised at you being so soft."

"I'm not soft!" Josie Smith said. "And I want to go on the roundabout! I want to!"

"Well, it's too late now," said Josie's mum. "You should have gone on before. Now, hold Eileen's hand. We don't want you getting lost."

Josie Smith walked next to Eileen but she didn't hold her hand. She hated Eileen for saying she was frightened of falling off the horse.

The wind started blowing hard again and the sun went in. Josie Smith felt a big raindrop slap on her cheek.

"If it starts raining," said Eileen's mum, "we'll go in the inside market before we look at the coats. We could do with a cup of tea."

Josie Smith hated the inside market. The stalls were so high up she couldn't see anything, and anyway there was only horrible meat and black puddings and fish. And the worst place of all was the café where they had cups of tea. It was noisy and you got pushed and there was too much talking and smoke. Josie Smith didn't want it to rain. She looked up at the sky as they walked along. There were a lot of dirty raggedy clouds up there and the wind was blowing them fast across the pale blue sky. Then a hard shopping basket hit Josie Smith on the ear.

"Look where you're going," said Josie's mum, pushing her forward. Grown-ups are always telling you to look where you're going but they never look down themselves, they just bang into you. The flaps on their coat pockets poke you in the eye, their coat buttons snap at your nose, their bags push you out of the way, and sometimes they even wheel prams over your toes. Josie Smith was fed up.

"Your mum says you've to hold my hand," Eileen said.

"Well, I'm not," Josie Smith said, "and you never saw me crying either."

"Gary Grimes was crying," Eileen said. "He's soft."

"So what?" said Josie Smith.

"Jo-sie!" Their mums were shouting. "Eil-een! Stop where you are a minute!"

When they looked round their mums were standing with a lady in a blue headscarf. They were talking again!

"I know what," said Eileen. "Let's go and stand over there."

"What for?" said Josie Smith.

"Because it's that stall where they have brooches with your name on."

"We're supposed to stand here," said Josie Smith. "Our mums said."

Josie Smith didn't want to get lost. She had

got lost once at the seaside and it was frightening. She stood where she was and Eileen ran off to the brooch stall. When she came back she was wearing a white brooch with "Eileen" written on it in deep pink letters and a pink and green flower at one side.

"It was only twenty pence," said Eileen. "I've bought a hairslide with a butterfly on it as well."

Josie Smith looked at the brooch and felt in her pocket for her ten pence. She hadn't been on the roundabout and now she couldn't buy a brooch. She felt in her other pocket just in case but there was only a toffee paper and some fluff.

Josie Smith held the ten pence tight inside her pocket and thought about the brooch. Then she thought that she hadn't been on the roundabout so perhaps she could ask her mum for her roundabout money. Only, when you ask for things you're pestering. She looked at her mum and Eileen's mum and the lady in the blue scarf. They were talking hard. Josie Smith wondered what to do. Sometimes when you pester your mum and she's talking she gets mad. But sometimes, when she's talking really hard, she gives you what you ask for without taking any notice. Josie Smith decided to try.

"Where are you going?" Eileen said.

"To ask my mum for ten pence," Josie Smith said.

"I'm asking mine as well, then," Eileen said, and she went too.

"You'll spoil everything," Josie Smith said, "if you start pestering." But she couldn't stop her.

Eileen ran up to her mum shouting, "We want ten pence! We want ten pence!"

"Don't interrupt," said Eileen's mum. "Can't you see we're talking?"

Josie Smith didn't say anything, but her mum said, "What have I told you about interrupting when people are talking?"

"I haven't interrupted," said Josie Smith. "I haven't said anything."

"It's all right," said Eileen's mum. "They want to buy something off that stall. I'll treat them." And she gave Josie Smith and Eileen twenty pence each.

"What do you say?" said Josie's mum.

"Thank you very much," said Josie Smith.

Josie Smith and Eileen ran to the brooch stall, pushing each other and giggling.

The brooches with names on them were pinned on to a large sheet of white cardboard and there were hundreds of them all in rows. The girls' brooches were all like Eileen's, white with pink writing and a flower. The boys' ones were dark blue with white writing and a little car instead of a flower.

The lady on the stall had a big fur coat on and a wholly hat with grey curls poking out and gloves with no fingers. She had purple lipstick on and some bits of leftover red nail varnish.

Josie Smith looked at her and said, "Can I have a brooch with Josie on it?" Then she remembered and said, "Please."

"They're all there," the lady said, "in alphabetical order. Do you know your alphabet?"

"Yes," said Josie Smith.

"Help yourself, then," the lady said. She turned away from Josie Smith and started talking to an old lady who was sitting down behind the stall.

Josie Smith started looking for her name. She saw Hilary and Helen and Iris and Irene and Janet and Joan and Jennifer. Then she saw Katherine and Kate and Lucy and Lydia and Mary and Margaret and Nina and Nancy. She must have gone past Josie. She started again from Hilary and Helen right down to Nancy but she still didn't find it. Perhaps somebody had picked it up to buy it and changed their minds and put it back in the wrong place. So she looked everywhere. She saw Alice and Barbara and Cathy and Denise. She went right to the end and saw Una and Vera and Yvonne and Zoe. But she didn't find Josie.

"Your name's not there," Eileen said. "I'm buying a bangle, are you?"

How could her name not be there?

"Excuse me," Josie Smith said to the lady in the fur coat, and she held her twenty pence so hard it hurt her hand. "Excuse me."

"Have you found what you want?" the lady said, holding out her hand for some money without looking at Josie Smith.

"No," said Josie Smith. "My name's Josie and I can't find it."

"If it's not there I haven't got it." Then she looked at Josie Smith. Josie Smith stared at her hard, wanting her to say she would find it. Perhaps it was behind the stall. Perhaps there was another whole card and her brooch was on that.

The lady said with a kinder voice, "They don't make everybody's name, love. It's just luck if you find yours. Choose yourself a nice bangle like your friend."

Eileen bought an orange bangle with glitter in it. Josie Smith was too upset to choose a bangle. Why didn't they make everybody's names? There were hundreds and hundreds of names there. They made Eileen's name. She looked again to make sure but it was just the same. Janet, Joan and Jennifer.

Another girl, bigger than Josie Smith, came to the stall with her mum and her mum said, "Look, Katy, there's a brooch with your name on it."

"I don't want it," the girl called Katy said. "I want a red Alice band."

"Jo-sie!" Their mums were shouting. "Eileen!"

They were going to look at coats. Eileen was holding her mum's hand and showing her the bangle and pestering for what she could have next.

Josie Smith held her mum's hand and her legs felt tired and people kept pushing her and she was fed up with the market. She wanted to go home. She wanted Percy and she wanted her wellingtons because the wind felt cold on her legs.

"Come on," said Josie's mum, pulling her along. "I thought you liked going to Christine Penny's stall."

"I do," said Josie Smith. But really she

didn't like it so much any more.

When they got there she couldn't see Christine Penny. Eileen started trying coats on. She tried a pink quilted coat and a sky blue one and a white one. Then she started crying and arguing with her mum. Josie's mum and Christine Penny's mum were talking. Josie Smith looked up at all the coats and jackets hanging above her head. Then she closed her eyes and sniffed the new clothes smell. Then she opened her eyes and read all the big signs written on white paper with red felt tip.

"Come here a minute," said Josie's mum. She was holding out a dark green quilted jacket with a big *Bargain! £££££s off!* label stuck to the back.

"I don't like dark green." Josie Smith said. "I like the ones Eileen's trying on."

But Eileen was still crying and shouting and Josie's mum carried on talking to Christine Penny's mum while she got Josie's arms through the sleeves and so nobody heard her. It was a horrible coat and even though she had it on over her other coat it was still miles too big.

"It's miles too big," said Josie Smith.

"You'll grow into it," said Josie's mum. "I'll turn the sleeves up." She tucked them up now.

BARGAIN!!!
££££sOff!

"Can I have a pink coat like Eileen?" asked Josie Smith. She didn't say the green coat was horrible because Christine Penny's mum was there and they were her coats.

"I'll give you pink!" said Josie's mum. "You'd look well in a pink coat digging for worms at Mr Scowcroft's. You'd have it ruined in five minutes. Turn round."

Josie Smith turned round and her mum pushed and pulled at the horrible coat from behind and said. "Stand up straight and hold your shoulders back." Then she started talking to Christine Penny's mum again. Josie Smith stood there with her back to everybody and her face near the coats hanging up and a big lump came in her throat to make her cry. She hated the great big horrible jacket and its dirty green sad colour so much that she wanted to throw it on the floor and stamp on it. But she didn't. She just stood there. Then the row of coats on a rack in front of her nose opened up and Christine Penny's face looked through the gap at her.

"I'm glad you've come," Christine Penny said. "D'you want a toffee?"

Josie Smith nodded and Christine Penny's face disappeared again. Josie Smith pushed through the coats and came out in the little space between Christine Penny's stall and the next one where there were more coats. Christine Penny was standing there with a bag of toffees.

"They're red," she said, "and if you rub them on your lips they make lipstick." She had her bangle on but she didn't have plaits today, she had a curly pony-tail. Josie Smith wished she had a curly pony-tail but her hair wasn't long enough. It wasn't curly either.

"Do you want to play hide-and-seek?" Christine Penny said.

Josie Smith nodded and Christine Penny said, "Shut your eyes and count to ten." And she started twirling Josie Smith round and round until they were both giggling. Then she ran away.

Josie Smith went on twirling round and giggling and counting and when she got to ten she opened her eyes. She pushed through the coats in front of her and ran past the back of the stall where someone was trying on a jacket and out through the coats at the other side. Christine Penny wasn't there.

Josie Smith pushed back in through the coats and she was just running round the front of the stall when somebody got hold of her and a man's voice shouted, "Here! What do you think you're playing at?"

It wasn't Christine Penny's stall. It was another stall like it. Her mum wasn't there and Christine Penny's mum wasn't there and Eileen and Eileen's mum weren't there.

"I'm talking to you!" shouted the man at Josie Smith. "What do you think you're playing at?"

"Hide-and-seek," whispered Josie Smith.

"Well, play somewhere else," shouted the man. "Go on! Hop it!"

Josie Smith turned away from the man and started pushing out through the coats but he came after her shouting, "Oi! Come here!

Where did you get that coat? That's not yours! Come back here, you little monkey, or I'll have the police after you!"

But he couldn't catch Josie Smith. She ran as fast as lightning, round and round and in and out between the stalls. When she stopped after a long time her chest was burning and she could hardly breathe.

"Aher! Aher! Aher!" she went. She was too frightened to cry so she just stood there going "Aher! Aher! *Aher!*"

When she did get her breath back she looked around to see where she was but she didn't recognize anything. That man had made her get lost. Why did he say the coat wasn't hers? She looked down at the horrible green coat. Perhaps he could tell because it was too big. Perhaps it was because it was open and he could see she had her own coat underneath. Josie Smith started walking along, trying to find Christine Penny's stall or the brooch stall or the roundabout, or even the hot potato man. She had to find somebody she knew so they would help her find her mum. After she'd been lost at the seaside, her mum had told her, "If you ever get lost again, don't get in a panic and start crying. And when somebody asks you where you live, tell them your address properly. Don't just say 'Across from Mrs Chadwick's'."

Josie Smith walked along, swallowing hard to stop the lump in her throat from making her cry, and practising her address to herself, over and over. But what was the use of telling her address if her mum was at Christine Penny's stall? She saw a barrow that looked like the hot potato man's barrow but when she got close it was a different man selling roasted chestnuts.

"How many?" he asked her, holding a paper cone up.

"I don't want any," said Josie Smith, and she turned away.

The man laughed and shouted after her, "I didn't know there was a sale of little girls today!"

Josie Smith didn't know what he meant so she kept on walking, swallowing the lump in her throat and practising her address.

She heard some music and started running towards it. The roundabout! She'd found the roundabout! But when she got there she looked at the roundabout man and remembered how he'd shouted at her to get off. She stopped and wondered what to do.

The roundabout man saw her and said, "Up you get. I'm setting off."

"I don't want a ride," said Josie Smith, and she turned to go away.

The roundabout man laughed and shouted after her, "They're selling little girls off cheap today!"

Josie Smith didn't know what she meant so she kept on walking, swallowing the lump in her throat and practising her address. Her legs were shaky and she felt a bit sick as well but she didn't panic. She thought hard and remembered that the stall with the brooches was quite near the roundabout. If she found that, the brooch lady might know where Christine Penny's stall was.

When she found the brooch stall the lady with the purple lipstick remembered her.

"Back again, are you? Have you decided what you want at last?"

"I don't want anything," Josie Smith said. "I want to find Christine Penny's stall because my mum's there and I'm lost."

She waited for the lady to ask her for her address but she didn't. She said, "Christine Penny? Christine Penny? You don't mean Mavis Penny?"

"It's a girl called Christine Penny and she's got a bangle and plaits only she hasn't got them today, she's got a pony tail."

"That'll be Mavis Penny's little girl. Wait a minute, I'll show you."

The brooch lady came out from behind her stall. She bent over and turned Josie Smith round and pointed. "Now, go straight down here until you get to that man who's selling stuff out of a suitcase in the middle. Can you see him?"

"Yes," said Josie Smith. "Is he selling monkeys that run up and down a stick?"

"No, he's not," the brooch lady said, "he's selling purses. Now, don't go past him. Turn right and walk along and Mavis Penny's stall is the second to the last on your left. Have you got that?"

Josie Smith nodded and set off before she could forget it all but the brooch lady called her back and said, "Have you no manners? What do you say?"

"Thank you," said Josie Smith.

"That's better. And where have you got that coat from? It's not yours."

"I know it's not," said Josie Smith. "It's Christine Penny's mum's. I was trying it on when I got lost."

"Well, you look a right comic with that sign on your back. Go on, then, off you go."

Josie Smith set off again but now she could feel the crackling paper sign on the back of the horrible coat and she remembered that it said *Bargain! ~~£££££s off!~~* Then she remembered people laughing at her when she turned to go away. Then she remembered that man on the coat stall who said he'd have the police after her. He thought she'd stolen the horrible coat! Josie Smith walked along and her face was burning hot and she was nearly crying.

When she got to the man selling purses she

stopped. Did she have to turn left and go to the second stall from the end on the right? Or did she have to turn right and go to the second stall from the end on the left? She couldn't remember. She looked left, trying not to panic. Then she looked right, trying not to panic. Then she saw Christine Penny running towards her. Christine Penny was shouting something and pointing at her. Then she looked back and waved at somebody to come and pointed at Josie Smith again. Coming along behind her was a policeman.

Josie Smith panicked.

She whizzed round and ran away as fast as her legs would go and she was roaring with fright. She didn't see where she was going and she banged into shopping bags and the corners of stalls and other children and a pram and a dog. She fell and hurt her knee and got up and kept on running and roaring and shouting for her mum. Then she crashed into a man and he got hold of her.

"Now, now, now," the man said, "that's enough. You're all right now." And he started drying her face on a big folded handkerchief. "I suppose you're Josie Smith," he said. "Your mum's looking for you, do you know that? We met her not five minutes ago."

Josie Smith stopped roaring and looked up at the man but she didn't know who he was.

"You don't know me but you know my lad, Stephen, don't you?"

Standing next to the man was Stephen Taylor, Josie Smith's new red-haired friend from school.

"Your knee's bleeding," Stephen Taylor said. He was holding a net on a stick. Stephen Taylor's dad bent down and dried her knee with the handkerchief. It felt sore.

"Your mum will have to put some ointment on that," he said, and he tied the handkerchief round her knee.

Josie Smith waited for him to ask her for her address but he didn't.

"Come on," he said. "We'd better find your mum. I'll take you to the market superintendent's office and they'll make an announcement." He got hold of Josie Smith's hand but she snatched it back.

"I don't want to go," she said.

A big crowd was standing round watching and they all seemed to know who Josie Smith was. Somebody said, "It's that little girl they're looking for." Then somebody else said, "See, there's the paper on her back."

Then a lady bent down and said, "You have to go to the market superintendent's office, love, and they'll say your name over the loudspeaker and your mum will hear it and come and get you."

"I don't want to go," said Josie Smith. She didn't want them to say her name because the policeman would come and get her.

"You're not frightened of going in an office, are you?" asked Stephen Taylor's dad.

"Yes," said Josie Smith. "I don't want to." But she didn't want to explain to him about the coat and the policeman.

"Well," said Stephen Taylor's dad, "I'll tell you what we'll do. You stay with our Stephen and I'll go and get your name called out. Then when your mum comes I'll bring her to you. Will that do you?"

"Yes," said Josie Smith. Even if the policeman came, too, her mum wouldn't let him take her away.

"Right," said Stephen Taylor's dad. "What's your favourite place in the market?"

"The roundabout," said Josie Smith.

When the announcement was made, Josie Smith and Stephen Taylor were sitting in the red engine on the roundabout. They rang the bell as hard as they could and Josie Smith's mum came with Stephen Taylor's dad. The policeman didn't come. Every time she went past in the engine, Josie Smith looked hard at her mum and wondered if she'd get smacked. Her mum's face was red but she was talking to Stephen Taylor's dad and he was making her laugh. Josie Smith wasn't going to get smacked.

Stephen Taylor said, "It's great, that coat. It's the same as mine." And it was. "It's camouflage green," he said.

"What's camouflage green?" asked Josie Smith.

"It's what soldiers wear," Stephen Taylor said, "and you can get mud and grass and anything on it and it doesn't show. You can wear it when we go fishing for tiddlers. I'm wearing mine and my dad's got one as well. He's bought me this net and he says he'll take us to Reddisher Woods tomorrow. Have you asked your mum for a jam jar?"

"Yes," said Josie Smith, "but I haven't got a net."

"We'll go and get you one after," Stephen Taylor said. "They're on that stall over there and they're only thirty pence. Have you got thirty pence?"

Josie Smith was just going to say no but then she remembered that she had.

"We'll take some apples," Stephen Taylor said, "and some toffees and a bottle of pop."

"Can we have dandelion and burdock?" asked Josie Smith.

"If you want," Stephen Taylor said.

And so that Stephen Taylor wouldn't think she was soft, she said, "I wasn't crying before because I was lost. There was a policeman after me for stealing this coat."

"He wasn't after you," Stephen Taylor said. "Your mum asked him to try and find you. You're a good runner, though. Look, there's that soft girl who plays with you."

There was Eileen in her new pink coat and her bangle and her butterfly hairslide. And there was Eileen's mum standing next to Josie's mum and Stephen Taylor's dad.

Josie Smith and Stephen Taylor rode past them all in their engine, and Josie Smith, in her camouflage green coat — *Bargain!* ~~£££££s~~ *off* ! – and thirty pence for a fishing net in her pocket, waved and rang her bell.

COLLECT A JOSIE SMITH BOOK
FOR EACH COLOUR OF
THE RAINBOW

JOSIE SMITH

Josie Smith saves up for a birthday present,
runs away from home and steals a ginger cat.

JOSIE SMITH AND EILEEN

Josie Smith has a secret party, goes to sleep at
Eileen's house and wants to be a bridesmaid.

JOSIE SMITH AT THE SEASIDE

Josie Smith goes to the seaside, meets a friend
more horrible than Eileen and gets lost on the
sands.

JOSIE SMITH AT SCHOOL

Josie Smith gets in trouble with the headmistress, meets a princess and wants to be a fairy in the school concert.

JOSIE SMITH IN HOSPITAL

Josie Smith goes to a frightening house, starts ballet classes and has her tonsils out.

JOSIE SMITH AT CHRISTMAS

Josie Smith makes an angel for the school crib and loses it, goes to a fancy-dress party and wins a prize and then waits up all night for Father Christmas.